W9-DIB-579

Alfred Noble Library
32901 Plymouth Road
Livonia, MI 48150-1793
(734) 421-6600

19

You're a Good Sport, Miss Malarkey

Alfred Noble Library
32901 Plymouth Road
Livonia, MI 48150-1793
(734) 421-6600

NOV 2 0 2002

To my sister,
Ellen Decker,
school principal
extraordinaire,
and the growing
Decker family.
—J. F.

3 9082 08879 1671

Text copyright © 2002 by Judy Finchler and Kevin O'Malley
Illustrations copyright © 2002 by Kevin O'Malley

All rights reserved. No part of this book may be reproduced or
transmitted in any form or by any means,
electronic or mechanical, including photocopying, recording,
or by any information storage and retrieval system,
without permission in writing from the Publisher.

All the characters and events portrayed in this work are fictitious.

First published in the United States of America in 2002
by Walker Publishing Company, Inc.

Published simultaneously in Canada by Fitzhenry and Whiteside,
Markham, Ontario L3R 4T8

For information about permission to reproduce selections from
this book, write to Permissions, Walker & Company, 435 Hudson Street,
New York, New York 10014

Library of Congress Cataloging-in-Publication Data
Finchler, Judy.
    You're a good sport, Miss Malarkey / Judy Finchler and Kevin
O'Malley.
      p. cm.
    Summary: The children on a newly formed soccer team love their
coach, Miss Malarkey, who doesn't know much about the game except how
to make it fun, but the school principal and parents have other ideas.
    ISBN 0-8027-8815-7 — ISBN 0-8027-8816-5 (lib. bdg.)
    [1. Soccer—Fiction. 2. Sportsmanship—Fiction.
3. Coaching (Athletics)—Fiction.]
I. O'Malley, Kevin, 1961-ill. II. Title.

PZ7.F4956658 Yo 2002
[Fic]—dc21   2002023063

The illustrations for this book were created in watercolor and
colored pencil on 140-pound watercolor paper.

Book design by Sophie Ye Chin

Calligraphy by Martha Myers

Printed in Hong Kong

2 4 6 8 10 9 7 5 3 1

STAFF MEETING
Union issues and 'THE TEST'
Many of our members have
expressd discomfort with the
current events in education.
Union Rep. D. Manda Ourshara
will be on hand to discuss
the union position.
**FRIDAY NIGHT
AT UNION HALL**

**SOCCER
SIGN-UPS**

SEPT. 8

You can't win, if you don't play
So sign up today!!!!!!!!!!!

PTA MEETING

How to apply for
and win college scholarship
money for your elementary -
aged child.

PRESENTED BY:
Dr. I. Intendtoscareia
The doctor has helped
thousands of parents get the
kind of headstart that

SCORES On the
state-wide te

MATH
ENGLISH
GYM
MUSIC
ART

The state will be eli
the art portion of th
next year

You're a
Good Sport,
Miss
Malarkey

Judy Finchler
and
Kevin O'Malley

Walker & Company
New York

NOAH

Wonc there
A Turky name
Bob.
He koud drive
a car
    The End
    Ryan Scott

CONNOR

A Turkey was
watching TY
when his stepdad
brother took
the REmote
    Quinn

DARA

Since our minds are in good shape from all the learning and tests in school, our principal, Mr. Wiggins, says it's time to work on being fit. We're not just part of a school, now we're part of a soccer league. It's called YELS (Youngstown Elementary League Soccer).

Mr. Wiggins was our first coach.

He showed us how to head the ball.

But he had problems.

Mr. Fitanuff, our gym teacher, took over for him. Then at practice one day he was explaining the best way to corner kick.

But nobody could understand what he was saying.

WINNING Corner KICKS

YOU →
GOAL →
BALL →

So now Miss Malarkey is our coach. Mr. Wiggins always says she's a team player. She's real nice, but she says she doesn't know that much about soccer. That's okay with me. Most of the kids on our team have never played soccer before anyway.

Everybody has their own talents, says Miss Malarkey.
Sean runs really fast. He runs around and around and around.

Lauren can really kick the ball. She kicks it all over the place.

Josh never leaves his position. He finds really good bugs.

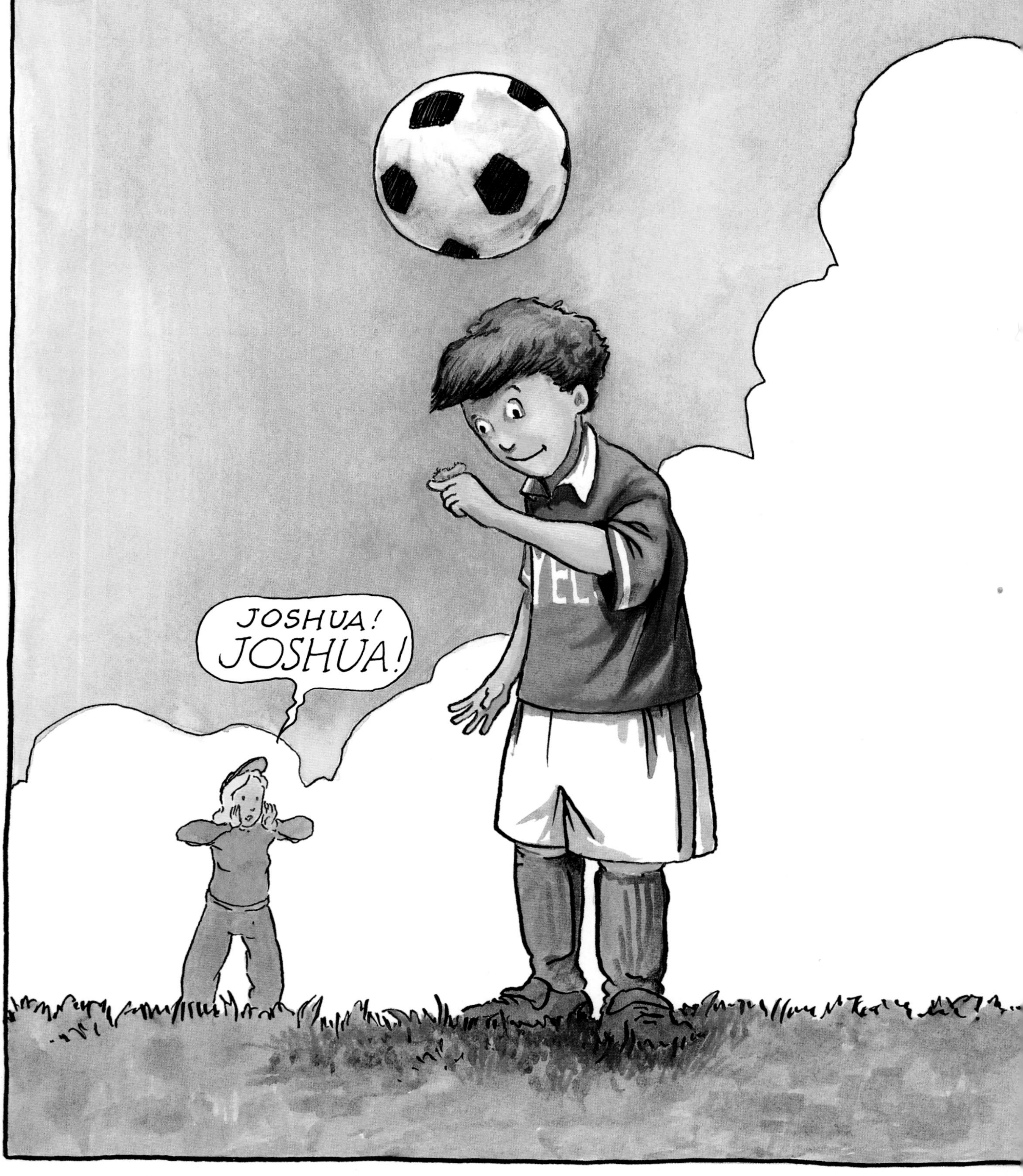

Patrick is really funny. He makes everyone laugh.

And Jason should have his own team. He dribbles really well.

We usually have a big crowd at our games. Most of the parents are there. Brothers and sisters get to watch too. Whenever grandparents come, they always get treated the best.

Katelyn's dad always comes late. Maya's dad and Justin's mom have phones attached to their ears. Sean's dad always worries about everyone on the team. And Tyler's mom is cool 'cause she brings snacks.

We have a lot of fun at practice.
Miss Malarkey is a fun coach.
We practice kicking the ball.

And how *not* to use our hands.

We play follow the leader.

But we still haven't won any games. So I guess the parents
are trying to help us, but they don't seem to be having much fun.
They're always yelling.

COME ON...
HUSTLE!

HEY, REF-
SHE WAS
OFFSIDES!

PASS THE BALL,
SHORTY!

On Friday Miss Malarkey called a team meeting. She told us how much better we've gotten. She said she was proud of us. And she said that at Saturday's game she wanted us to try our best.

Principal Wiggins called our team into his office the same day. He told us how important it is to win. Saturday's big game is against East Braggerly Elementary. "We have to beat Principal Wretchet . . . I mean . . . it's important to try your hardest to beat these guys."

Saturday's game started off really well. Everybody tried and nobody cried when they fell down or made a bad mistake. It was fun, but it was pretty weird because the parents were sort of quiet. They looked sort of nervous.

The trouble started after halftime when the other team scored a goal.

Principal Wiggins ran over to suggest a few plays.
Melissa's mom told Miss Malarkey that Melissa wasn't playing enough.

Jason's father started yelling for everybody to hustle. Sean's mom
said Jason was a ball hog. So Jason's mom started yelling at her.

The other team kicked the ball and it hit Jimmy and he fell down.
His parents ran onto the field and the referee called for a penalty shot.

That's when Sean's dad and Principal Wiggins ran onto the field. The other team's parents started yelling. Three babies and a grandpa who were napping woke up and started to cry. I mean, only the babies started to cry, not the grandpa.

Everybody was going nuts.
Miss Malarkey threw her soccer book into the air and yelled—

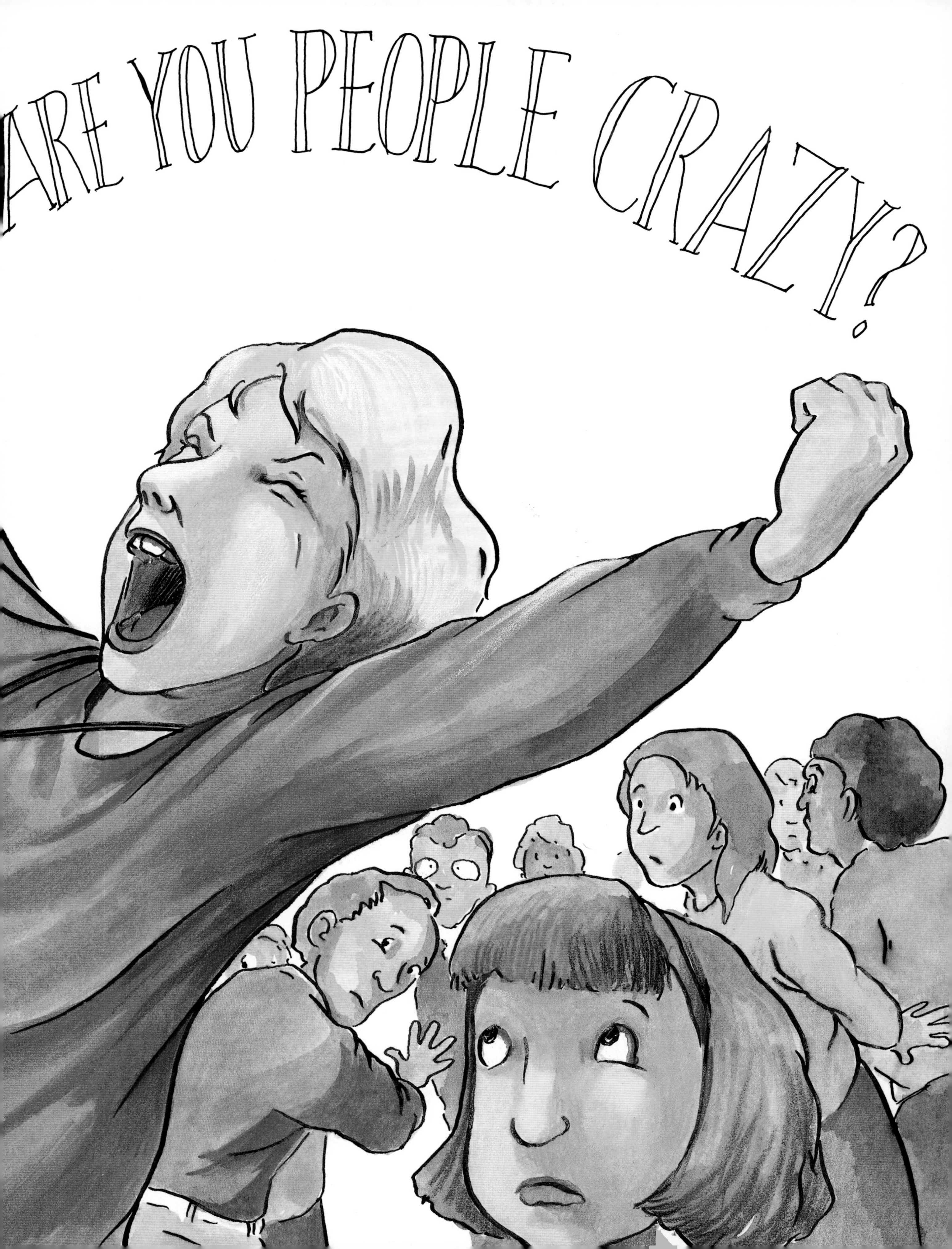
ARE YOU PEOPLE CRAZY?

They sort of had to cancel that game.

Things are different now. They changed the name of the league and everything. Instead of YELS it's now called SILENT (Soccer Instructional League, Elementary Neighborhood Teams). Parents aren't allowed to yell or cheer. They can only clap really politely.

All the parents are given lollipops before the games to help keep them from yelling.

Miss Malarkey is still our coach. She's really nice, and she hardly ever has to use her soccer book anymore.

Sometimes she still yells, though. She says it's important for everybody to try and remember—